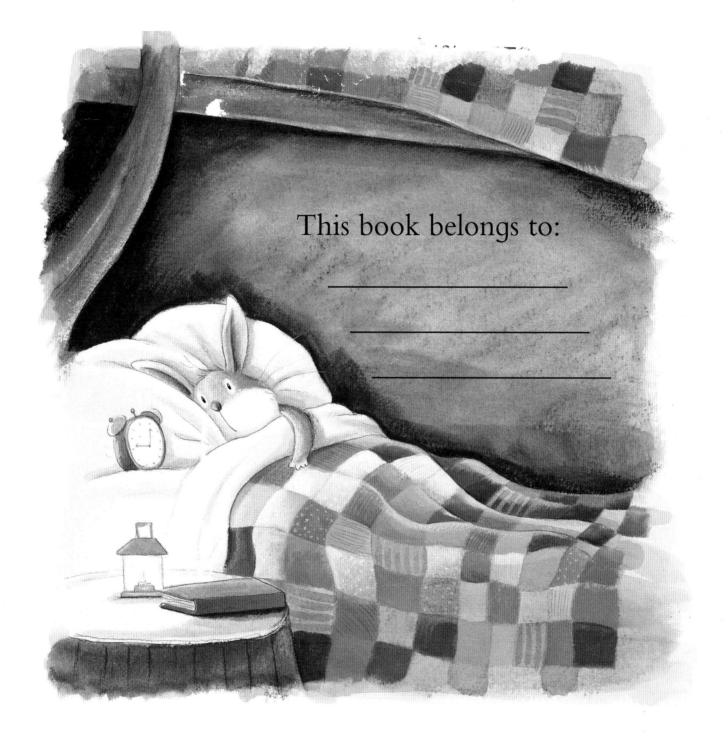

This book belongs to:

_____

_____

_____

For Stephanie ~ may she keep
on finding the right words ~ N.L.

For Isaac ~ T.W.

LITTLE TIGER PRESS
An imprint of Magi Publications
1 The Coda Centre
189 Munster Road, London SW6 6AW
www.littletigerpress.com

First published in Great Britain 2009
Text copyright © Norbert Landa 2009
Illustrations copyright © Tim Warnes 2009
Norbert Landa and Tim Warnes have asserted their rights to
be identified as the author and illustrator of this work
under the Copyright, Designs and Patents Act, 1988
A CIP catalogue record for this book
is available from the British Library
All rights reserved

ISBN 978-1-84506-851-6
Printed in China
2 4 6 8 10 9 7 5 3 1

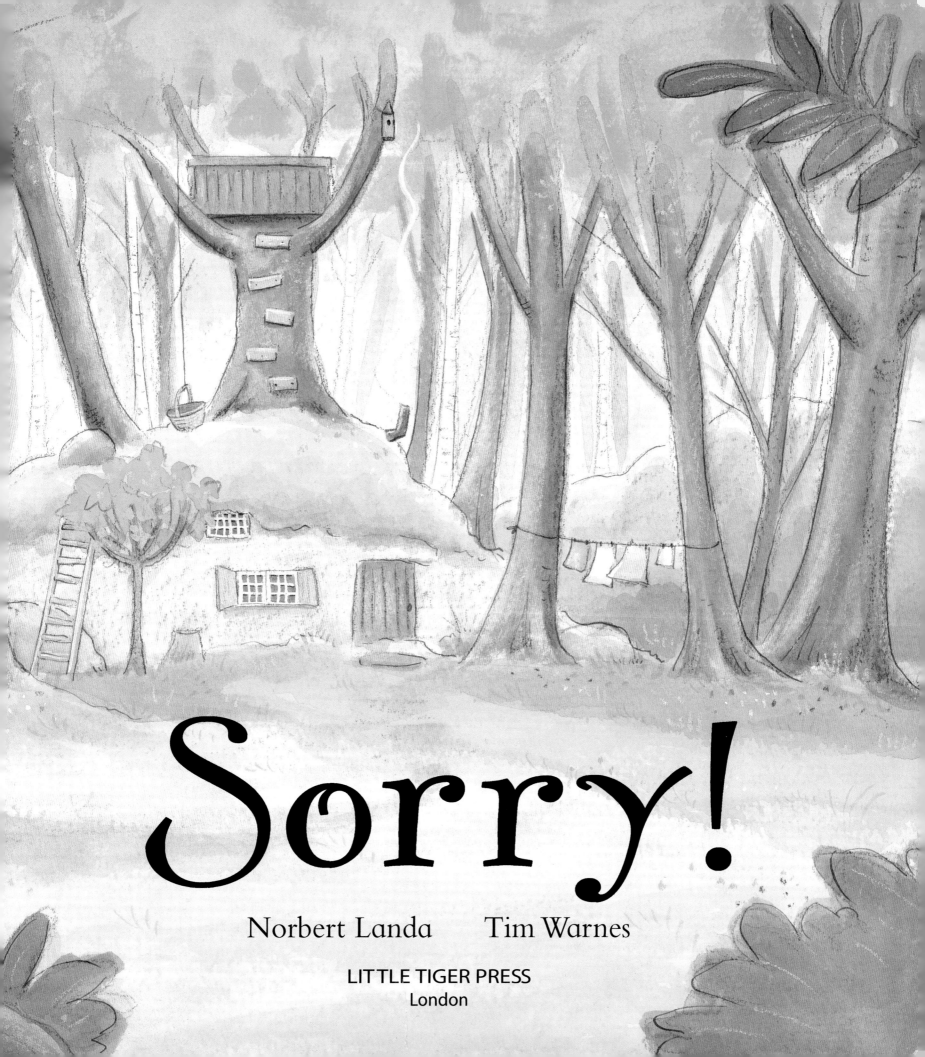

Sorry!

Norbert Landa Tim Warnes

LITTLE TIGER PRESS
London

Bear and Rabbit were the best friends
you can imagine.
They lived in their Bear-Rabbit house.

They cooked their Bear-Rabbit meals
in their Bear-Rabbit kitchen.
Rabbit was better at frying mushrooms.
Bear was perfect at making honey-cakes.

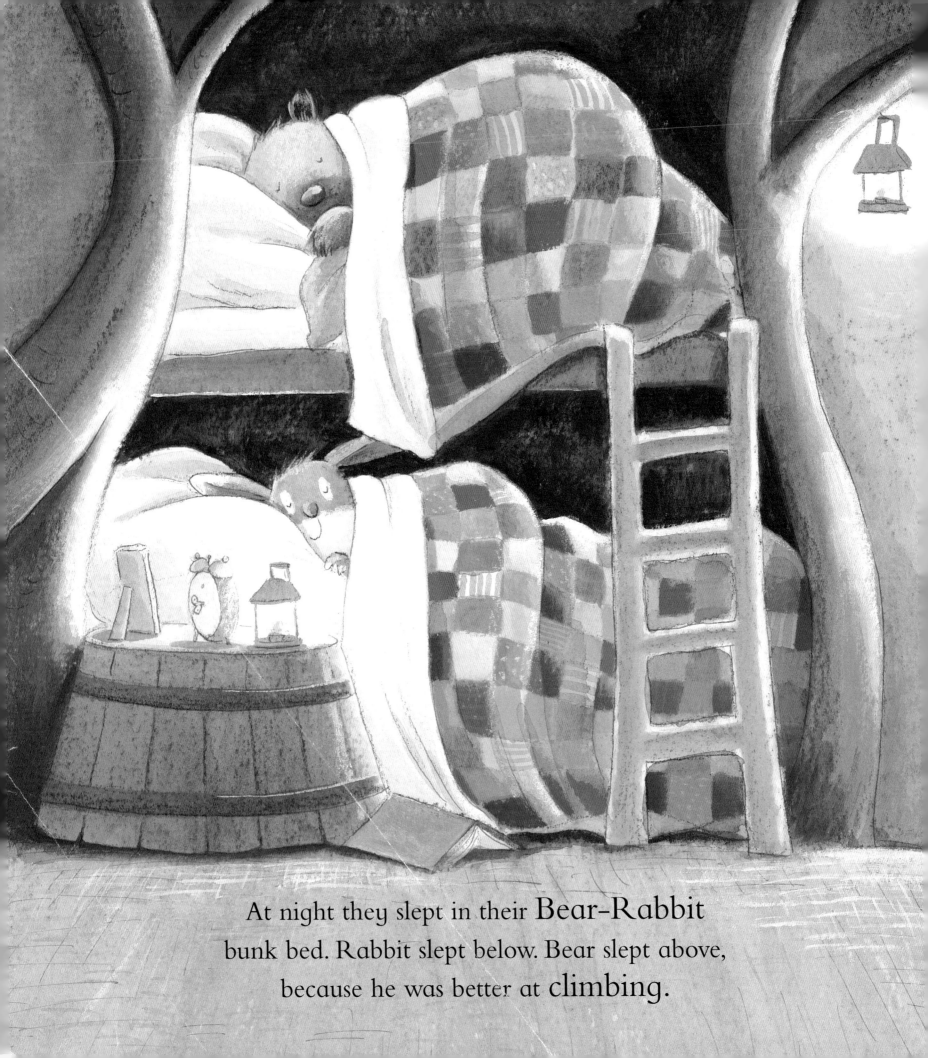

At night they slept in their Bear-Rabbit
bunk bed. Rabbit slept below. Bear slept above,
because he was better at climbing.

In summer they lived in their tree house.
Rabbit told stories to Bear, because he
was better at telling stories.

It was a wonderful feeling being a good
friend and having a good friend.

One summer morning, Rabbit saw
something **blinking** and
twinkling in the sun.

"**Look,** Bear!" he said.
"What's **that** down there?"

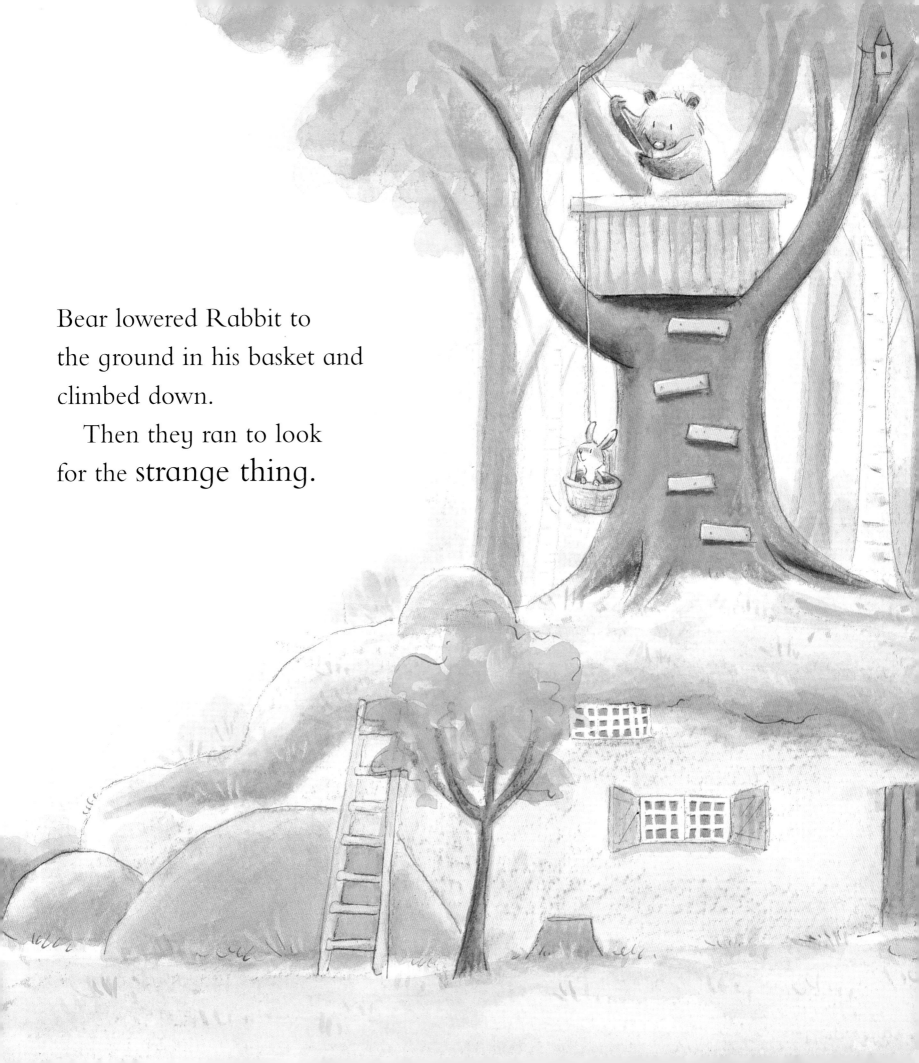

Bear lowered Rabbit to
the ground in his basket and
climbed down.

Then they ran to look
for the **strange thing**.

Bear went right up close and looked into it. He had never seen a thing so shiny!

"Goodness," he said. "It's a picture of me! Look, Rabbit. What fluffy Bear ears I have!"

So Rabbit looked into the shiny thing.
"You're kidding," he said. "It's a picture of me!
My pretty, long ears, don't you see them?"

"You are **completely** wrong," said Bear, grabbing the shiny thing. "These are small and round and fluffy **Bear** ears. This is **my** picture!"

Rabbit grabbed

and Bear pulled and

Rabbit pushed

and Bear t u g g e d.

And the two of them tore the shiny thing into two.

Then
they
both
stormed
off . . .

with

their

own

little

piece.

Oh, how **mad** Rabbit was! He strode back to Bear-Rabbit house and **slammed** the door.

Then he stuck the shiny thing to the wall, so he could look at his picture and **proudly** say,

"Wonderful, pretty, long ears!"

Then he went to bed. What else could
he do, alone in Bear-Rabbit house?

Meanwhile, angry Bear climbed up the tree house and stuck his piece to the wall.

He sat down on the bench, to admire himself and his round, fluffy ears.

Then he looked down to Bear-Rabbit house.

"I could really do without such a friend,"

he grumbled.

Evening came and night came. But Rabbit
could not sleep and he wasn't angry any more.
"How silly I was!" he sighed.
"How good it would be to have Bear
here with me, so I could tell him a
wonderful goodnight story."

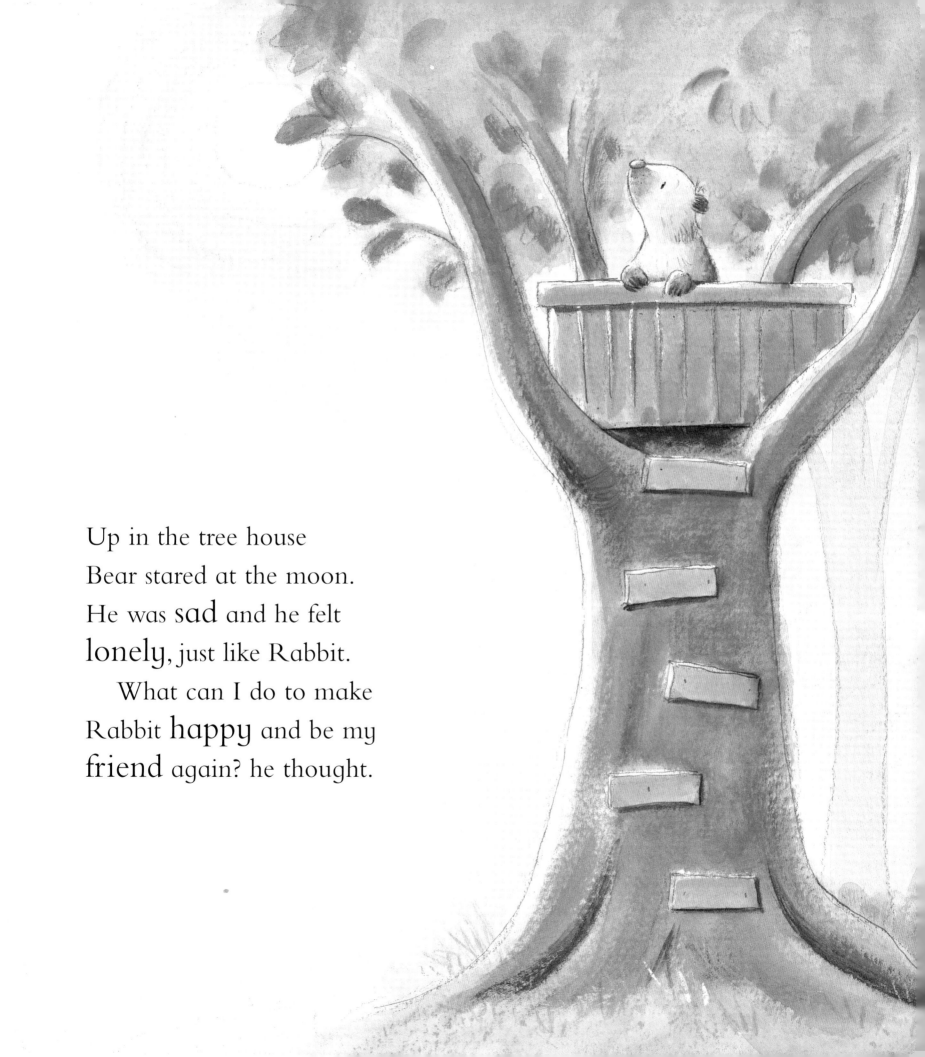

Up in the tree house
Bear stared at the moon.
He was **sad** and he felt
lonely, just like Rabbit.

What can I do to make
Rabbit **happy** and be my
friend again? he thought.

Then Bear had an idea. He took his
little piece of the **shiny thing**
and climbed down the tree.
Quietly he padded to
Bear-Rabbit house.

But Rabbit was not in bed, either.
He was standing outside, holding in
his hand his **own** little piece.

When he saw Bear, Rabbit walked towards
him and whispered, "Sorry, Bear.
You can have my picture!"
"Oh no, I'm sorry!" Bear said
and gave him his own.

But when they got into a huddle
and looked at the shiny things,
what did they see . . . ?

. . . a picture of both of them!

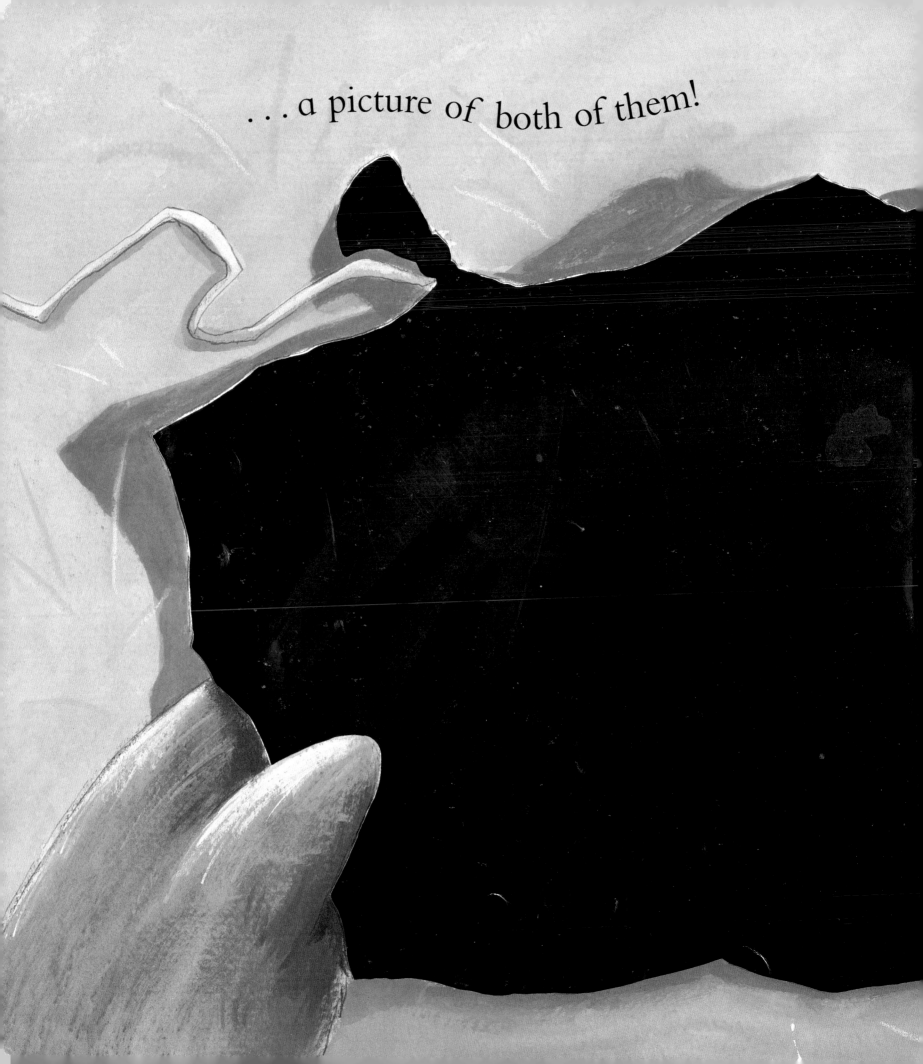

"That's just perfect!" said Bear and Rabbit happily.